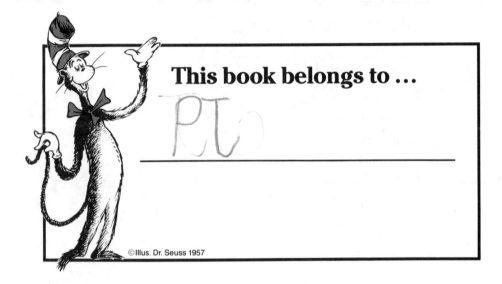

This book belongs to ...

PT

©Illus. Dr. Seuss 1957

IN A People House

by Theo. LeSieg

Illustrated by *Roy McKie*

A Bright & Early Book

RANDOM HOUSE / NEW YORK

"Come inside, Mr. Bird,"
said the mouse.
"I'll show you what there is
in a People House . . .

A People House
has things like . . .

. . . chairs

IN A People House

by Theo. LeSieg

Illustrated by Roy McKie

A Bright & Early Book

RANDOM HOUSE / NEW YORK

things like

roller skates

and stairs.

banana

bathtub

bottles

brooms

That's what you find
in people's rooms.

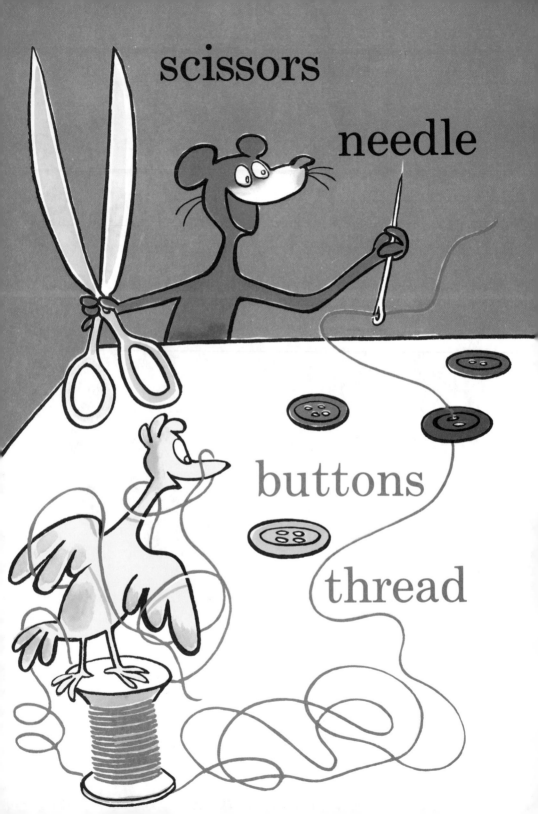

cup
and
saucer

pillow

bed

These are doughnuts.

Here's
a
door.

Come along, I'll show you more.

Here's a
ceiling

here's a **floor**.

piano

peanuts

popcorn

pails

Here's a **ceiling**

here's a floor.

piano

peanuts

popcorn

pails

pencil

paper

hammer

nails

salt and pepper

goldfish

key

table

telephone

TV

Come on!
Come on!
There's more to see!

You'll see a
kitchen sink
in a People House,

a shoe

and a sock

and a clock
said the mouse.

bread and butter

window

wall

toothbrush

hairbrush

big blue ball

baked beans

bureau drawers

and

books

lights and lamps

and hats and hooks

mirror

marbles

shirt

and string

knife fork spoon

and
bells
to
ring

doll

and

dishes

teapot

trash

And . . .

Another thing,
it's time
you knew . . .

. . . A People House
has people, too!

"And now, Mr. Bird,
you know," said the mouse.
"You know what there is
in a People House."